Text copyright (c) 2021 by Bobby Parrish and Dessi Parrish
Illustration copyright (c) 2021 by Kaloyan Nachev and Boril Nachev

All rights reserved. No part of these publications may be reproduced, distributed, or transmitted in any form or by any means, including photocopying, recording, or other electronic or mechanical methods, without the prior written permission of the publisher, except in the case of brief quotations embodied in critical reviews and certain other noncommercial uses permitted by copyright law.

Printed in the United States of America
ISBN: (p) 978-1-64250-739-3
(e) 978-1-64250-740-9
www.mangopublishinggroup.com
www.flavcity.com

The Tasty Adventures of Rose Honey
CHOCOLATE CHIP COOKIES

by Bobby & Dessi Parrish
Cowritten and Illustrated
by Kaloyan Nachev & Boril Nachev

The aroma of morning tea drifting
from the kitchen tickled the nose of Rose Honey.
And while she was still snuggled in bed,
eyes closed tight, she already knew exactly
what she wanted to do that day!

"Mommy! Daddy!" she called. "Let's make my favorite chocolate chip cookies!"

She popped out of bed, slipped on her apron, and climbed to the tip-top of her chef's tower. From above, she could see so many delicious ingredients spread out in front of her. She was the chef, and Mommy and Daddy were her helpers.

Mommy had already taken out the creamy butter, so it was nice and soft.
Rose sneakily pinched off a little piece.
Yum, yum!
It melted in her mouth.
A splash of vanilla extract.
Then the sugar.

Rose reached into a jar full of brown crystals. They were so sweet! Daddy called them coconut sugar.

Then she tasted the sparkling white crystals, but the salt quickly pinched her tongue. "A good chef always tastes along the way," confirmed Mommy.

To make the cookies chewy and delicious, Rose had lots of nutty choices.

Now came her favorite part. Cracking the eggs. Tap tap... Rose was excited, but oops! She cracked the egg so hard it spilled on the floor.
"Don't worry, just keep practicing," said Daddy.
"We'll clean it up together."

"Mommy, it's your turn!" said Chef Rose.
"Mix, stir, blend."
All the ingredients came together in one magical cookie dough.

While Mommy started rolling the dough into small balls, Rose began the most important task of all—placing the chocolate chips on top of the cookies. A chip for the cookie and a chip in her mouth.

Time to bake! The hands on the clock seemed to move so slowly! She kept peeking at the cookies through the oven door while she helped clean up. The smell of sweet vanilla and butter was filling up the whole house.

Hooray! The cookies have finally cooled!
Rose couldn't wait to share them with Mommy,
Daddy, and her Teddy. She took a bite.
Soft and chewy, warm and melty, yummy chocolate chips.
"We made a bit of a mess, but it was worth it!" said Daddy.
"Mmhmm," agreed Rose, her mouth full.

That night, when Rose went to bed,
she remembered the soft, warm cookies.
They felt just like Mommy's hug.
She dreamed of floating through the sky
and landing on the moon.

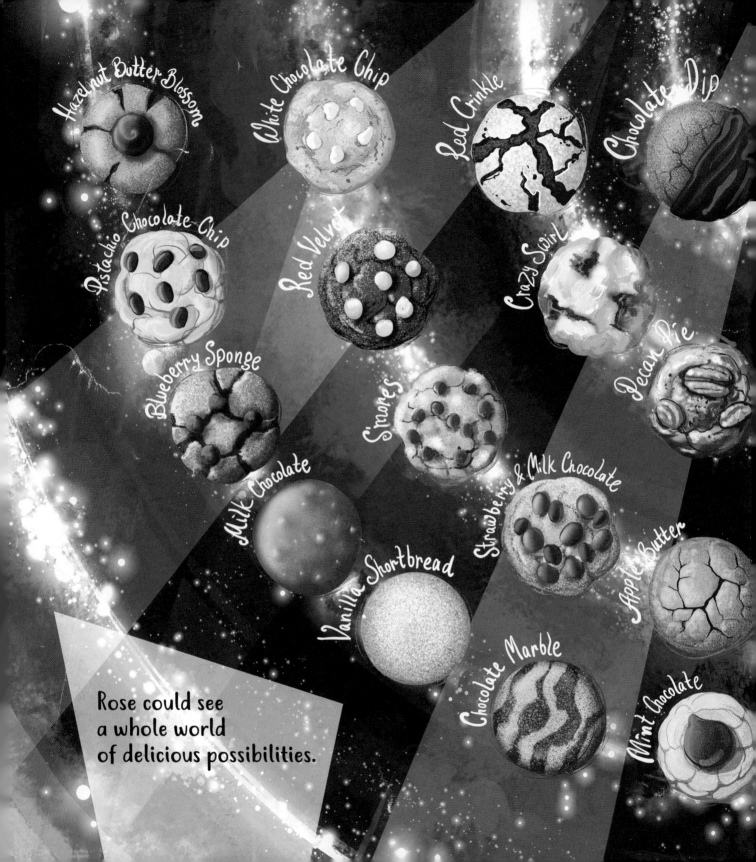

Rose could see a whole world of delicious possibilities.

The Cookie Planets

- Plain Chocolate
- Dark & White Double Chocolate
- Walnut & Chocolate
- Pumpkin Crinkle
- Vanilla Dream
- Double Chocolate
- Chocolate Chip
- Strawberry & White Chocolate
- Chocolate & Coconut
- Almond & Coconut
- Salted Caramel
- Peanut Butter
- Rainbow Dash
- Lemon Curd

TeaWay Galaxy

Constellation Teacup

Rose Honey could not wait to make something yummy again tomorrow.

← Rose's Home

TeaWay

Teapot Constellation

Chocolate Chip Cookies

PREP TIME: 15 MINUTES
COOKING TIME: 13 MINUTES
MAKES: 18 COOKIES

INGREDIENTS:

- ⅔ cup (75g) almond flour
- ½ cup (60g) arrowroot or tapioca starch
- 2 tablespoons (20g) coconut flour
- 1 teaspoon (5g) baking soda
- ¼ teaspoon salt
- 1 stick (½ cup/113g) unsalted, grass-fed butter (or ghee/coconut oil), room temperature
- ½ cup plus 3 tablespoons (108g) coconut sugar
- 1 teaspoon (5ml) vanilla extract
- ⅓ cup (90g) creamy almond butter (or peanut butter/cashew butter/pecan butter)
- 1 pasture-raised and organic egg
- ¾ cup (140g) paleo or sugar-free chocolate chips

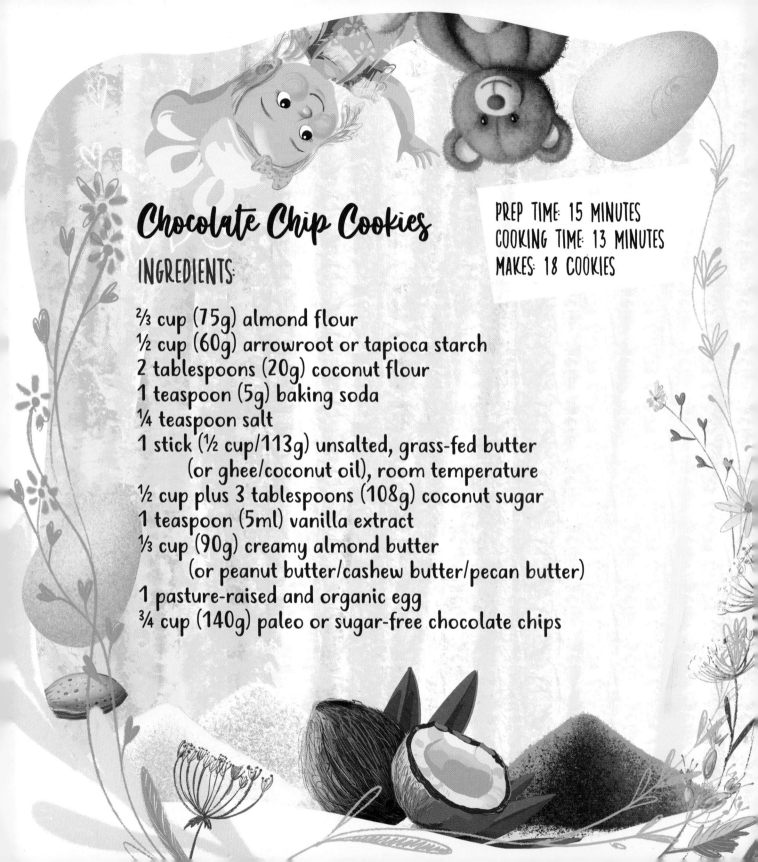

DIRECTIONS:

If you don't have the first three ingredients, you can buy Bob's Red Mill paleo baking flour mix from the store and use 1¼ cups (160g) of it for this recipe.

To a medium bowl, add the first three ingredients (or the paleo mix) as well as the baking soda and salt. Mix well and set aside. In another bowl, beat the butter, sugar, and vanilla together for about 3 minutes on high using a hand mixer. Add the almond butter and beat on medium for another 30 seconds to combine. Add the egg and beat just to combine.

Add the dry flour mix to the wet ingredients and stir with a spatula until thoroughly combined. Add the chocolate chips and mix well. Alternatively, you can add the chocolate chips to the cookies once they are on the sheet tray. Cover the batter with plastic wrap and chill for at least 30 minutes in the refrigerator or overnight.

Preheat the oven to 350°F (175°C) and line a sheet tray with parchment paper. Use a cookie scoop or spoon and place dough a few inches apart on the sheet tray. You will have more dough than can fit on one sheet tray. Bake for about 11 to 13 minutes or until lightly golden around the edges. Let cool on the sheet tray and enjoy!

Watch Rose Honey make these delicious chocolate chip cookies!

JOIN THE TASTY ADVENTURES OF ROSE HONEY IN OTHER BOOKS AS WELL

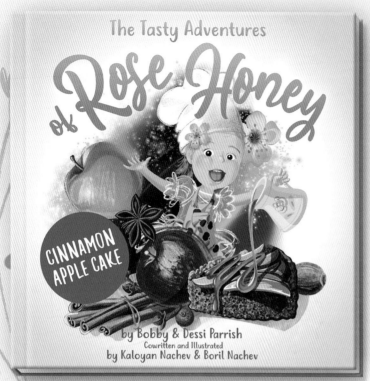

CINNAMON APPLE CAKE

Rose finds herself in the land of flavors and aromas. On her journey, she learns many things and preparing a delicious cake is one of them.

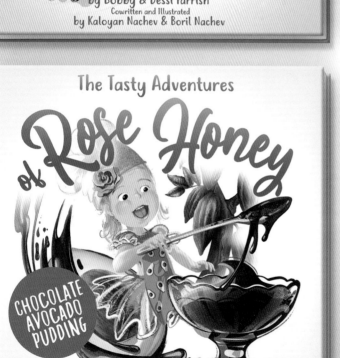

CHOCOLATE AVOCADO PUDDING

While making her special chocolate pudding, Rose finds out about the magic of growing up and how the little seed turns into a big tree.

ABOUT THE AUTHORS

Bobby and Dessi are bestselling cookbook authors with millions of followers across the world. With his popular FlavCity videos, Bobby shares grocery shopping and healthy food tips. Bobby's favorite place is in the kitchen, making delicious meals for his family.

Dessi dedicates her time to raising their daughter, Rose Honey. She also enjoys paleo baking, doing food photography, and painting.

Rose loves being involved in everything Mom and Dad do, especially in the kitchen where she helps make all kinds of tasty dishes. You can find all of Rose Honey's cooking videos on the FlavCity Facebook page. www.facebook.com/flavcity

ABOUT THE ILLUSTRATORS

Kaloyan Nachev, the illustrator and cowriter of this book, is also Dessi's brother. He is an acclaimed artist, producer, director, and screenwriter. He lives in Bulgaria where Dessi is originally from. Kaloyan has four children and loves spending time with his family. His oldest son, Boril Nachev, helped cowrite and illustrate this book. Kaloyan adores his niece Rose Honey and has a special connection with her, as she was born just a few days after his youngest daughter Petra.